For Finbar
and Jock

Copyright © 1994 by Flora McDonnell

All rights reserved.

First U.S. edition 1994
Published in Great Britain in 1994
by Walker Books Ltd., London.

Library of Congress Cataloging-in-Publication Data

McDonnell, Flora.
I love animals / Flora McDonnell.—1st U.S. ed.
Summary: A girl names all the animals she
likes on her farm, from Jock the dog to the
pig and her piglets.
ISBN 1-56402-387-7
[1. Domestic animals—Fiction.]   I. Title.
PZ7.M478434Iaac   1994
[E]—dc20   93-2463

10 9 8 7 6 5 4 3 2 1

Printed in Belgium

The pictures in this book were done in acrylic and gouache.

Candlewick Press
2067 Massachusetts Avenue
Cambridge, Massachusetts 02140

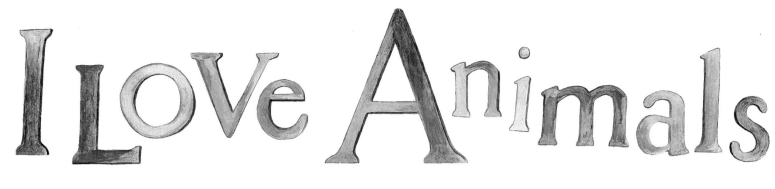

I LOVE Animals

Flora McDonnell

CANDLEWICK PRESS
CAMBRIDGE, MASSACHUSETTS

I love Jock, my dog.

I love

the ducks

waddling to
the water.

I love the hens
hopping up
and down.

I love the goat

racing across
the field.

I love the donkey

braying
"hee-haw!"

I love the cow
swishing her tail.

I love the pig with

all her little piglets.

I love the pony

rolling

over

and

over.

I love the sheep
bleating to
her lamb.

I love
the cat

washing her
kittens.

I love the turkey

strutting

around

the yard.

I love all
the animals.

I hope they love me.